Jim,

Hide and Seek

by

Catherine MacPhail

Based on the blurb by

Becky Wright

Catherine MacPhail
June 26
2009

First published in 2009 in Great Britain by
Barrington Stoke Ltd
18 Walker Street, Edinburgh, EH3 7LP

www.barringtonstoke.co.uk

ISBN: 978-1-84299-658-4

Printed in Great Britain by Bell & Bain Ltd

This book is based on the following blurb written by Becky Wright of Morgan Academy, Dundee.

The school was dark. Empty. Phoebe and her five best friends sat alone in their Maths classroom, getting ready for a ghostly game of hide and seek. One after another they start to go missing. Will they be able to find their friends in time to face the danger that hovers around the corner?

From Catherine MacPhail

The Dundee Project. Such an exciting idea for a competition. Pupils from the high schools in Dundee were asked to write a blurb for a book, and what a fantastic prize there was for the winner. To have a real book written from your blurb. Wow!

I wanted to write the book for this competition. When I come up with an idea for a book, I nearly always write it as a blurb first. I start work on writing the book from there. But this is the first time I've written a book from someone else's blurb. We had over 1500 entries, and I read every one of them.

Hide and Seek was the winning blurb. Becky Wright sent it in and I liked it right away. It had everything a good story needs. A haunted school, a group of friends, one by one they go missing. As soon as I read the blurb, I could see where I could have cliff-hangers, suspense and lots of scary moments.

I hope I've done a good job. Hope I keep you turning the pages, hope I send a shiver up your spine, and perhaps give you a few surprises too. I am so proud to have been part of this project!

From Becky Wright

There were so many people that went in for the competition to write a blurb that Catherine MacPhail would turn into a book. I still can't believe that I'm the one that won. When I think that the book will be in shops and libraries all over the country, it doesn't seem real. The blurb I wrote started out with me thinking about what it would be like to play hide and seek in a school.

Now it's grown into a book with the help of lots of people. I had other little ideas but I thought that the ghost story would make the best story. The book that Catherine MacPhail has written is better than I could have ever imagined. There are loads of stories out there about ghosts or children at school – but the way that Catherine MacPhail twisted this story is great. It's just amazing to think that I get to be part of a book that will stay in libraries across Britain next to thousands of other books. I'm so lucky to have won and I'm very grateful for the chance of a lifetime.

This book is dedicated to
two wonderful Dundee librarians,
Moira Foster and Stuart Syme,
without whom it might never have
been written.

Contents

Chapter 1
The New Girl

"Is this school really haunted?" the new girl asked.

Nicola looked at her and smiled. "Sorry, I've forgotten your name again," she said.

"Destiny," the new girl said. "My name's Destiny."

Of course Nicola hadn't forgotten at all. How could anyone forget a name like Destiny?

What had her parents been thinking of when they gave her such an odd name? This new girl, Destiny, was pale and plain and boring. She was in none of Nicola's classes. She had only started in the school this week. Nicola had spotted her walking from one class to another as if she was lost. Or stupid. Nicola didn't know which. Mmm ... perhaps the name did fit her. There *was* something odd about her.

Nicola kept on smiling. "Sorry, what were you asking, Destiny?"

"Someone told me this school was haunted. Is that true?"

Nicola had heard the stories too. That in the dead of night, floor-boards creaked in empty class-rooms, chairs were lifted and dropped. Doors that had been locked suddenly opened. People said some evil spirit lurked in the dark of one class-room. 1C.

Nicola didn't believe any of the stories. They were all rubbish. But she wasn't going to tell Destiny that.

Instead, she whispered to her, "They say if you dare to stay in here all night, the evil that lurks here will come to you."

Destiny looked ready to explode. Her pale eyes grew big. "Has anyone ever done it? Stayed in the school all night?"

And as soon as Destiny said that, Nicola began to think of a plan. And Destiny was going to walk right into it. "I wouldn't have the nerve," Nicola said quickly. Then, after a moment she added, "Would you?"

Before Destiny could answer, Danny came across to talk to them. Nicola tried not to let her heart skip. But it was hard. He was *so* good looking. Thick floppy dark hair and the brownest eyes she had ever seen. She was sure he must like her too. She was just counting the moments till he asked her to the school disco.

He smiled, and her heart did flip then. She couldn't stop it.

"Hi!" he said, with a grin. "What's going on here?"

"Destiny wants to stay the night in the school. Even after I told her people think there's a ghost. Isn't she brave?"

Nicola stepped behind Destiny's back and winked at Danny. He was as quick as she was. He knew right away what she was up to. They both saw things the same way. Oh, they were meant to be together, her and Danny!

Destiny went red. "Oh, but I never ... that's not what I ..." she tried to say.

Danny cut in. "But that's a great idea. I've always wanted to find out if those stories are true." He shouted over to his best pal and another girl who were walking past. "Sanji, Marianne – want to spend a night in a haunted school?"

Marianne jumped at it. "I'd love it!" *Of course she'd love it*, Nicola thought. Marianne was after Danny too. She was always fluttering her eyelashes at him, and giggling at every little joke he made. Well, any trouble from her and Nicola would find some handy locker to shut her into. Good way to get rid of her.

But the chance to spend the night in the school with Danny? It was a dream come true. And if Nicola had to pretend that she was scared so that Danny'd put his strong arms round her, so what? She'd put up with having wimpy Marianne there too. She'd think of a way to lose her.

"I can say I'm staying over at Soo's," Marianne said, and called her best friend, Soo, over.

Nicola was annoyed – Danny, Marianne, Sanji and now Soo. How many more people were going to be there? This wasn't what she planned at all. "Are we inviting the whole school?" she said crossly.

Danny winked at her. Her heart flipped again. "No, just us ... and Destiny, of course," he said.

Destiny's face was still brick red. *She must be so chuffed that she's with a cool crowd like us*, Nicola thought. *She wouldn't dare say no.*

At last, Destiny smiled. "OK," she whispered.

Nicola slipped an arm around her as if Destiny was her new best friend. Boy, they were going to have some fun with the new girl.

Chapter 2
Nicola's Plan

It was all planned for Friday. The cleaners left early on a Friday, and the care-taker was off to a wedding. Danny knew that because his brother sometimes did odd jobs for the school. And Danny, clever, handsome Danny, had found out how to turn off the alarms.

"What are you up to, Nicola?" Danny asked her on Friday morning. They were all sitting in the school cafe. All of them ... but not Destiny.

"What makes you think I'm up to anything?" Nicola said.

But Danny was smart. Almost as smart as Nicola. "You're always up to something. What nasty little plan is it this time?"

"Oh, come on, Danny," Nicola said. "We can scare the socks off the new girl. Destiny!" The name still annoyed her. She deserved all she got with a name like that.

Nicola looked around at the others. "And I expect you all to join in and do something to scare her."

"Creepy noises in another room ..." Soo giggled.

"Doors that creak open." That was the best Marianne came up with. *A bit weak*, Nicola thought.

But it was Sanji who had the best idea. "Someone goes missing. They go off alone, and they don't come back ... and we can't find them, no matter how hard we try."

"Fantastic!" Nicola said. But she had to add to it. "And then, we all go missing, one by one." She giggled. "Until Destiny's all alone in the dark. That will really freak her out."

Her smile vanished when she saw how close Marianne was to Danny. Nicola planned for *her* to be the first one who went missing.

"Do *you* think the school's haunted, Danny?" Marianne asked. She was fluttering her eyelashes so fast she was making a hurricane.

"Better not be," Danny laughed. "Or I'll be the one that freaks out."

"You don't believe all that junk?" Nicola snapped at Marianne.

"Do *you* believe it, Nicola?" All of a sudden Destiny was there, as if she'd come from nowhere.

Nicola jumped. "Woah, Destiny, you gave me such a scare."

"Are we still on for tonight?" Destiny's voice trembled. She was ready to back out, and Nicola was having none of that.

"Don't say you don't want to go, Destiny," she said. "I mean, it *was* your idea."

Destiny shook her head. "Oh, no, I'm not going to back out. It's going to be fun, isn't it?"

"It's going to be a scream!" And Nicola started giggling, and couldn't stop.

Chapter 3
Night School

It was Sanji who found a way into the school. *Sanji would make a great burglar,* Nicola thought. He could find a way in anywhere.

It was almost ten o'clock when they got there. It was pitch dark, apart from the moon flitting in and out of the fast-moving clouds. The high wind made the trees sway back and forth as if they'd come to life.

"Great night for a ghost hunt," Sanji said, and Nicola saw Marianne take a step closer to Danny.

"I'm so glad you're here, Danny," Marianne giggled. Danny smiled at her, and it seemed to Nicola that his white teeth sparkled in the moonlight.

"You like him, don't you?" Destiny asked her.

Nicola gave a shrug. "He's good looking, I suppose."

"Yes, he is," Destiny said.

Nicola glared at her. Not that she had to worry about Destiny. *She* was no threat. She didn't stand a chance with Danny. She was too dull. Too boring. There was no life in her at all.

Sanji was inside the school. He opened one of the windows on the ground floor. "Hey, come on, you lot. Someone will see you if you stand there any longer."

Soo was in first. Sanji made sure of that. Those two could never stay apart for long.

12

Then it was Destiny's turn. She was wearing stupid clothes. Hardly dressed for a night in the school. Why was she wearing a dress, for goodness' sake, on a night like this? And those silly high heels. Everyone else had trainers on. Who was she trying to impress?

Nicola waited till last. Till the new girl and Marianne had climbed in, and only Danny was left. Then she acted as if she needed Danny to help her. That was a joke. Nicola didn't need anyone. But he liked looking after helpless little Marianne. So Nicola could be helpless too, if she had to be.

Danny held her back. "What have you got planned for in here?"

Nicola opened her bag, and lifted out a Halloween mask. The face was weird and ugly.

"She won't fall for that," Danny said.

"Bet she will ... when it's dark ... and she's all alone."

"You're bad, Nicola," he said. And to Nicola, it sounded like a compliment.

The corridors were dark and silent. The trees scratched against the high windows. They padded along and made no noise. The only sound was the clip of Destiny's heels. "Who is it that haunts this school, anyway?" she asked in a whisper.

"You can guess," Soo told her. "The ghost care-taker. The dead teacher. There was a fire a long time ago. One of the teachers died in it. And now, the care-taker roams the corridors, night after night."

"Did he feel bad because someone died?" Destiny asked.

"Not exactly. It was him – the care-taker – that started the fire. Seems him and the teacher had been having a fling and she dumped him. The fire was his way of getting his own back on her ... he made sure she was locked in the class-room. The dead teacher roams round the school too, looking for him."

Nicola had to make the story even more creepy. "And they say if you get one look at her ..." She looked into Destiny's face. Her voice became a whisper. "You go mad. Because she has no face left."

At that moment a door rattled. They all jumped. Destiny screamed. Soo moved closer to Sanji and he laughed.

"Oh, Sanji, was that you?" Soo giggled.

"If it works this well, I'm going to rattle doors all night," Sanji said.

"Where are we going?" Destiny asked.

Nicola slipped an arm in hers. "To the English corridor. Class-room 1C. That's where the teacher was trapped. It's the room where all the creepy things happen."

"The school's spooky at night, isn't it?" Marianne said to Danny, as they began to go up the stairs.

Marianne was keeping far too close to Danny. Nicola didn't like that. She'd have to do something about that.

There were no carpets on the stairs and all they could hear was the clatter of Destiny's silly shoes. There were photos of the old headmasters on the walls. Their eyes stared down. They didn't look happy.

"Look at that one," Danny said. "I think he's watching us."

And it did seem as if the headmaster's grim stare never left them.

"They don't look so scary in the day-time," Destiny said. She stopped and stared at the photo and bit her lip. She looked as if she was about to run home.

Out of the darkness a hand reached out and rested on her cheek. Destiny screamed. She almost tripped and fell back down the stairs.

Nicola stepped out from the shadows. She was still wearing the rubber hand.

"Goodness, Destiny, you almost had a heart attack then," Nicola said. Destiny was shaking. She was never going to last the whole night in here, if a silly Halloween hand could scare her like that.

The English corridor was on the first floor. Sanji pushed open the swing doors and they followed after him. It was a long corridor with tall windows on one side that looked down into a little garden the pupils had dug and planted. On the other side of the corridor was a long line of class-rooms and lockers.

"1C is right at the end," Marianne said. She began to run. Her soft shoes made no sound on the floor. Her voice echoed down the empty corridor. "Sanji will have to pick the lock to get us inside."

At the class-room door she stopped dead. Stepped back. She let out a gasp.

"What's the matter?" Nicola shouted.

But Marianne didn't have to answer.

They could all see what the matter was. The door of 1C was wide open.

Chapter 4
The Haunted Room

"Do you think the door was locked?" Destiny asked. She was out of breath. She'd been the last to catch up with them. Couldn't run in those silly shoes.

They were all standing round the class-room door. "Of course it was locked," Nicola said. "All the class-rooms are locked at night." Then she added in a scary voice, "The dead care-taker must have opened it."

Sanji took out a little box of tools. "I'm good at picking locks," he said, "but I didn't pick this one."

But then, as Destiny looked away, Nicola saw a wicked grin flit across Sanji's face. Of course he'd picked it. Part of the fun.

"Maybe the care-taker just forgot to lock it today," Destiny said. She sounded hopeful. "His mind would be on that wedding he was going to."

"Yes, I bet that's it." Soo put a comforting arm around her.

They all stepped into the class-room, one by one. 1C seemed different in the dark. They'd sat here so often, as the teacher droned on, while the rain hammered on the windows and the wind blew. Just like tonight. Their teacher loved Shakespeare and there were posters all over the walls of *Hamlet* and *Macbeth*. There was even a picture of a ghost out of one of those plays. A skull sat on the desk too. It made them laugh during the day, in the light. Only now it looked spooky. Did it glow? Or was that a trick of the moonlight that suddenly darted out of the clouds?

Nicola gave herself a shake. What a load of rubbish! She was here to have fun, not to fall into the trap of thinking any silly ghost story was true.

"What are we going to do now?" Sanji asked as he closed the door. "Sit here and wait for a ghost?"

"Please don't anyone say, 'let's have a séance!'" said Destiny. It was her idea but as she said it, her voice trembled.

"I like the sound of that." Marianne giggled. "You know, sit in a circle, join hands, and call up the dead."

Danny held out his hand to her. "I'm up for that."

Marianne grasped it and giggled again.

The wind seemed to get even louder. It was banging at the windows, as if it was trying to get inside.

It hadn't been part of her plan, but maybe a séance was a good idea. "Let's do it!" Nicola said.

"Oh, no, please! I'd be too scared," Destiny said.

Nicola ignored her. "First we'd better sit down."

Nicola pretended to trip and bump into Marianne so that she got pushed away from Danny. It worked and that was exactly what Nicola wanted. Now, Danny was next to *her*. In the séance, it was her hand he was going to hold.

They all sat on the floor and made a circle.

Nicola took a deep breath. "Is there anyone there?" she called out softly into the darkness.

Danny tried not to giggle. Destiny just looked nervous.

"The ghost isn't talking to us," Soo said.

"The ghost won't come till midnight," Nicola said. She'd just made that up. For all she knew the ghost walked round the school all night long. But midnight sounded good, and she saw Destiny shiver when she said it. "We have to wait." She drew in a deep breath. "If there is anyone there, give us a sign," she called. Her voice was soft. "Spirits of the school ... are you there?"

A moment passed, a moment when no one made any noise.

"Oh, come on, you silly old ghost!" Danny shouted and they all laughed. "Don't be stupid. Give us a sign, for goodness' sake!"

And then they heard it, way off on another floor, another corridor. Music that moaned its way up through the empty school.

23

"I know that tune," Soo said. "It's an old Scottish song. *Will you no' come back again?*"

Sanji jumped to his feet. "That's a mobile phone."

"I thought there was no one else in the school?" Destiny said.

"There isn't," Soo said.

"Then whose phone is it?"

As suddenly as it began, the music stopped.

"I'm going to get that phone," Sanji said. "Someone's left it here by mistake. They're ringing it so as to try to find it. There's nothing scary at all. Back in five."

Soo tried to hold him back. "Don't go, Sanji," she said.

But nothing was going to stop him. He waited for a second at the door, and gave Nicola a look. *One of us goes missing*, he'd said. That had been his idea. He was going to be the first to go. Nicola smiled at him. He'd planted that phone earlier, she was thinking. Then, just now, he'd rung it from his own phone. All part of his plan.

Sanji saw her smile. After a moment, he nodded. Yes, it was Sanji.

Nicola looked at Destiny. Her face was deathly white. "I think the séance was a really bad idea," she said.

Chapter 5
The Message

"Shouldn't we go and look for Sanji?" Destiny stood at the smartboard. "He's been gone more than five minutes."

Nicola saw her chance to get rid of Marianne. "Why don't you go, Marianne?"

Destiny took a deep breath. "I don't think we should split up."

She wishes she hadn't come, Nicola thought. Nicola could see the fear in her eyes.

"Why don't you phone him?" Destiny said.

"I was just going to say that." Nicola was a bit annoyed that it was Destiny who'd come up with that idea.

It was Soo who pulled out her phone first. After a moment she looked up. "I don't have any signal."

One by one they all took out their phones. None of them was working.

"But ... if you can't get a signal," Destiny asked, "how come we heard a mobile phone ringing a moment ago?"

Even Nicola didn't have an answer to that one.

"Destiny's right," Marianne said. "Let's all go and look for Sanji."

In a way, Nicola was glad. She wanted to get out of that class-room. The wind was battering the windows. They rattled, and any moment she was sure they would shatter. The wind was so strong that, even with the windows shut, the posters on the walls rippled as if they were coming to life. If she sat here for any longer, in the dark, doing nothing, she really would begin to think the place was haunted.

Nicola was the last one out. "I'll leave the door open. When we find Sanji we'll come back here."

The long English corridor was full of dark shadows. No one moved.

"Sanji?" Marianne called out his name, and her voice rang out into emptiness.

Destiny shouted. "There! Someone's there, in the shadows."

Nicola tried to look. There was nothing. It was just Destiny seeing things. Or was it?

Nicola winked at Soo. Was this another part of Sanji's plan? Did Soo know what Sanji was going to do next? But Soo was just as puzzled as Nicola. She gave a shrug.

It had to be Sanji. And Nicola wasn't going to spoil his fun. She grabbed Destiny's hand. "I think I do see something down there. Let's find out!" She began to run, dragging Destiny behind her.

Destiny tried to pull her hand free. Nicola wouldn't let go. And then they were all running. Running and laughing and yelling for Sanji.

But not Destiny.

She was screaming. Screaming with fear.

They ran to the end of the corridor, to the swing doors. Nicola pushed at them, but the doors stayed shut.

"They're locked," Danny said. "How come they're locked?"

It was then Nicola saw that Danny still held Marianne's hand. It was her hand Danny should be holding. Why hadn't she grabbed *him* when she began to run? Why had she

29

grabbed hold of stupid Destiny? She pushed between Danny and Marianne so they had to break apart. "Must have been Sanji," she said.

"But where is he?" Destiny sounded scared. "Why didn't he answer us? He must have heard us shouting."

"Never mind where's Sanji." Now it was Danny who sounded scared. "Where's Soo?"

****

They stood in a circle. Back to back. Calling out her name, again and again. But there was no answer.

"Soo, this isn't funny any more," Marianne shouted.

Nicola wanted to tell Marianne that this had all been part of the plan. First one of them would go missing, then another. Only now, here in the dark, it didn't seem funny at all.

"She must have run into one of the class-rooms," Danny said, and he began to hurry back up the corridor. He tried to open each door in turn. They were all still locked. Even the fire door at the other end of the corridor was locked. The only door that still lay open was the door of 1C.

"She has to be in here, hasn't she?" Danny looked back at them. "Bet they're both in here."

But there was no Soo and no Sanji. They tried the door of the cupboard in the class-room but no matter how they pulled it, it wouldn't open. "I don't like this," Marianne murmured.

Nicola wanted to tell her to shut up. This was all working perfectly. The way they'd planned. Destiny was standing alone, nervous and hugging her arms round herself. Sanji and Soo had probably hidden in one of the locked class-rooms. Sanji could get in anywhere. Didn't Marianne remember that?

Suddenly Destiny let out a cry of fear. She was staring at the smartboard. "Look! Look!"

They all looked at the words lit up there.

Be afraid, Nicola. I'm coming.

Chapter 6
Be Afraid

The only sound was the howl of the wild wind outside.

At last someone said something. "Why is it after you, Nicola?" asked Destiny.

Nicola didn't understand that herself. Why was her name written on the smartboard? Why didn't it say **Be afraid, Destiny**?

It was Destiny who was the one they were meant to be freaking out. Nicola's name on the smartboard was not part of the plan.

She ran to the smartboard and rubbed at the words. "This is …" she started to say. She almost blurted out, "This is Sanji's idea of a joke," but stopped in time.

Even thinking that made her feel better. That was what had happened. Sanji had darted in here while they were all running up the corridor, and he had written on the smartboard. And now where was he? With Soo? He knew the school really well. He'd know where to hide.

A séance, weird sounds, a warning on the smartboard. All the sort of stuff they giggled about on sleep-overs. Nothing really scary about them at all.

Danny began to laugh. "Bet him and Soo are snuggled up somewhere, snogging," he said.

Marianne giggled. "Sounds good to me."

Even in the dark of the class-room, Nicola was sure she saw Danny blush. He wouldn't, couldn't, prefer ugly old Marianne to her. Not in a million years.

"You're not scared, Danny?" Destiny asked.

"No. Soo and Sanji are doing all this to scare us," he said.

"It's a mean and cruel game to play on anyone." Destiny looked back to the smartboard. Only one word was left. **Coming**. "Nicola must be so scared."

Her! Scared! Nicola snapped back at Destiny, "It's part of the joke!"

"It's a joke?" Destiny was stunned. "Have you played jokes like this before?"

The wind seemed to die in that instant. There was only silence in the class-room. "Of course we haven't," Nicola said. She looked at Danny quickly, then at Marianne. She was trying to stop them from saying anything.

"No, of course not," Marianne said. "We never have."

There was a shadow on the glass panel of the class-room door. It flitted over the glass. It moved fast and then an instant later, it was gone.

"There's Sanji," Danny said. He called out his name.

"It's only the trees," Destiny said.

Danny ran to the door. Called out Sanji's name again. But there was no one there.

The doors at the end of the corridor were not locked now. They could hear them, in the darkness swinging back and forth.

"That had to be Sanji," Danny said. "I'm going after him."

Marianne tugged at his arm. "No, don't go."

Danny looked at her. Another second and Nicola could see him and Marianne going off

together and then they would be the ones
snogging in some cupboard. No way!

She clung to Marianne's arm. "You have to
stay here, Marianne. With us."

"This is just like those films you see."
Destiny seemed to be talking to herself. "One
by one they vanish, and never come back.
Until there's only one left." She looked at
Nicola. *"Be afraid. I'm coming, Nicola*, it said.
Why you, Nicola? There must be a reason."

Nicola was getting really fed up with the
new girl. They'd wanted to scare *her*, not the
other way round.

Destiny moved back against the wall. "And
it's not even midnight," she said. "So ... what's
going to happen then?"

And in just that second it came again. The
spooky tune from the mobile phone,
somewhere in the school. *Will you no' come
back again?*

"I want this to stop." Marianne's voice shook.

Danny patted her arm. "Sanji's going a bit too far. I'm going to get him."

And before they could stop him, Danny was off and running, down the corridor, and through the swing doors.

The three girls watched them swing back and forth. Back and forth.

"He won't come back again," Destiny whispered. "I bet he won't come back again."

Chapter 7
The Game

Five minutes passed. Or was it more than that? Still no Danny.

This wasn't the way Nicola had planned it. They could all vanish, but not Danny. Her plan was for her and Danny to be tucked together somewhere in the school, hidden from Destiny, while Destiny ran from here to there, scared stiff, looking for them.

Marianne stood at the door. Watching for him. Calling for him. "Danny!" Her voice was carried on the wind, along the corridor, and all through the empty school.

"I told you he wasn't coming back," Destiny said again.

Nicola snapped at her. "Shut up!"

Marianne turned round sharply. "Did you tell him to go, Nicola? Was this part of your plan?"

Destiny stood up. "What do you mean, did Nicola tell him to go? Is he hiding?"

"Shut up, Marianne." Nicola's voice held a warning.

But Marianne didn't care. "Of course he's hiding. Haven't you got it yet, Destiny? It's all a game."

"Shut up, Marianne!" Nicola stepped forward. She didn't want Marianne to say anything else.

"A game?" Destiny asked. "What kind of a game?"

Marianne stared at Nicola, as if she was thinking what to say next. Then she shook her head. "We wanted to scare you, Destiny. We were going to spend the night in the haunted school, and do everything we could to scare you."

Destiny sat down quickly on a desk. "You mean … they're not missing at all? They're just hiding somewhere, laughing at me?"

"Yes! You asked for it, Destiny," Nicola said. They had to tell her now. It had all gone wrong anyway. "'Is this school really haunted?' you said. 'Has anyone stayed the night here?' You were a nightmare waiting to happen."

"This was all your plan? The mobile phone going off, the locked doors, the words on the smartboard?"

Marianne pointed at Nicola. "It was Nicola's plan. It was all her. It's always all her."

"And of course you said no!" Nicola snapped back. "Just like you didn't say no the last time."

Destiny's voice was a whisper. "The last time? Have you done something like this ... before?"

Nicola was fed up with this. She stepped forward. "*She* asked for it too."

"She?"

"The other girl," Marianne said softly. "Lana Watt. I've always felt so bad about what we did."

Marianne sounded as if she was going to cry.

"What did you do to her?" Destiny asked.

Nicola tutted. "Nothing much. She was crazy already."

"No, Nicola, admit it. We were so mean and cruel to her ..." Marianne let out a sob. "We drove her crazy."

Destiny stepped back from them into the shadows, as if she was afraid of them both. "You drove her crazy?"

"It was too easy," Nicola said, she was *not* going to feel bad about it. "It was fun. She couldn't take a joke. We'd tell her she'd done something, and she hadn't. But we all said we'd seen her doing it, and in the end she believed us.

Or we'd tell her she'd been somewhere and she hadn't. Then we'd take her to the place and, surprise, surprise, there'd be something she'd left behind."

Nicola glared at Marianne. "And you all were a part of it. Don't say you weren't. Danny rang a few times to ask Lana out, and she'd wait and wait, and he didn't turn up and then he'd say he never called her at all. And

43

don't forget, Marianne, you were the one who put the stolen locket in her bag."

It was a clever plan, Nicola remembered. She'd gotten the idea from an old film. A man driving his wife crazy, making her believe she did things that she hadn't. Until she went totally mad.

They hadn't expected Lana Watt to take it so badly.

"We were amazed when Lana said she had stolen the locket," Marianne said. "She found it in her bag and after everything else that had happened, she really did think she must have stolen it."

"She was just stupid," said Nicola.

"She had a *breakdown*, Nicola. She still can't go to school. That was our fault." Marianne slumped into a seat. "Someone in her family had died, and she hadn't gotten over it ... and we just made it all worse for her."

"How were we to know that?" Nicola was angry with Marianne. "She would have had a breakdown anyway. It had nothing to do with us."

"You said you were her friend," said Destiny. "Did you never think of how bad you must have made her feel, day after day? Did you never think how you must have hurt her?" It was as if Destiny couldn't believe what she was hearing.

"I've always felt bad about what we did," Marianne muttered.

"But not so bad that you couldn't do it again tonight," Destiny said.

Marianne couldn't even look at her. "I'm so sorry, Destiny."

"How could you all could be so cruel?" Destiny began to walk to the door. "I'm getting out of here."

Marianne tried to hold her back. "No, Destiny. You'll get lost in the school. You don't know your way about in here."

Destiny pulled away from her. "I'd rather be lost and alone than here with any of you," she said. "You make me sick!"

She was gone before they could stop her. "Let her go," Nicola said. She glared at Marianne. "You shouldn't have told her anything."

Chapter 8
And Then There Was One

Destiny's foot-steps clattered down the corridor. *She'll trip in those heels*, Nicola was thinking, *and serve her right*. They listened as she pushed her way through those swinging doors.

"We should go after her," Marianne said.

"Let her go. She'll get lost." Nicola giggled. "She'll really be scared then. We'll hear her screaming in a minute."

Why was Marianne looking at her like that? As if Nicola was something that had just crawled out from under a rock?

"Why are you always so cruel, Nicola?"

"It never bothered you before," Nicola snapped back at her.

"Yes it did," said Marianne. "But I was too much of a coward to go against you."

"You shouldn't have told her!" Nicola stabbed a finger into the darkness as if Destiny was still standing there. "Not about Lana Watt."

"I'm going after her," Marianne said.

"Go then. See if I care. This was meant to be fun. It was Sanji who went too far. The mobile phone, the words on the smartboard ..." The memory of those words made her shiver all over again. Why *had* Sanji written her name and not Destiny's? He shouldn't have done that.

"All that must have been your idea," Marianne said. "Sanji wouldn't do all that by himself."

"I didn't tell him to do anything!" Nicola shouted. But Nicola could see that Marianne didn't believe her.

"It's finished, Nicola." Marianne said. "The game's over."

"It's not over till I say it's over." Nicola stood her ground. She wasn't running off like a scared rabbit.

Just then they heard a cry from somewhere on another corridor. A cry of terror.

"Help me! Oh, somebody, please ... help me ..."

Then all was silent again.

Marianne was shaking. "Was that Soo?"

The cry had scared Nicola too. Who was it?

"Maybe it was Destiny," Marianne said.

"I said we'd hear her screaming in a minute," Nicola said.

Marianne looked at her as if she was going to be sick. "What sort of person are you, Nicola? Why was I ever friends with you?" She ran into the corridor. "I'm going to find the others." She shouted, "Destiny? Soo? I'm coming!"

And then she was gone.

Nicola listened to the sound of her soft foot-steps getting further away. *Let them all go*, she thought. She didn't need anyone. In a moment, she would walk out of the school, head high. She wasn't running away like Marianne. She wasn't scared.

Who had screamed out there? A scream of terror, as if they'd just seen something terrifying.

She tried to tell herself it was only Destiny, who had lost her way. Perhaps she'd fallen down the stairs in her silly shoes.

But what if it was something else?

Nicola was alone now.

This wasn't how she wanted it to end. It was Destiny who was meant to be alone.

Alone in the class-room at midnight, when the ghost walked. Then Nicola had planned to really let her have it. The weird mask, foot-steps closing in on her, maybe shutting her in one of the lockers for the rest of the night.

Nicola jumped when a shadow moved beside her.

Her own shadow!

How stupid she was being.

A poster rippled on the wall. The poster of the ghost from *Macbeth*. It was as if it began to move, the face came to life, the eyes watched her.

Stop it, Nicola. Get a hold of yourself, she thought.

Just then, she heard the doors in the corridor swing open. Someone had come back. Marianne?

She ran to the class-room door. "Marianne. I knew you'd come ..."

The corridor was empty. It seemed to stretch deep into darkness. But the doors were swinging, back and forth.

"Who's there?" Her voice sounded odd. "Marianne," she shouted, "is that you?" Only silence. "Danny?"

What had happened to all of them? Where were they?

Nicola was getting angry. She began to run. She was going to find them.

No one was going to scare her!

Chapter 9
Alone

She had never known the English corridor was so long. It seemed to stretch forever into blackness. Blacker than black. She felt the way you do in a dream, that she was moving but never getting anywhere. The doors seemed to be as far away as ever.

It was all in her head. She took a deep breath, and made herself stay calm. She stopped running. She would walk slowly towards the doors, push them open, go down the stairs and leave the way they came in.

At the top of the stairs she stopped again. Had something moved down there? Or was that the shadows of the trees outside?

"Marianne? Is that you?"

It had only been a shadow that she'd seen move down there. She was sure of it now. One step after another. She tried not to look at the photos of the long-dead headmasters that stared down at her.

Then she heard it. A soft humming sound. What was that?

Nicola stopped dead. She was hardly breathing. The humming became a whirr as it came closer. Any second now, she'd see what it was, see what the sound was coming from.

Then she saw.

The buffer was sliding on its own over the floor. Nicola had seen it often enough when the school care-taker cleaned and polished the floors. But here it was with no one pushing it along. Nicola shouted, "Who's there? Who's doing that?"

But there was no answer. Just the buffer, working its way back and forth, heading for the bottom of the stairs. Closer and closer it came. Nicola couldn't look at anything else.

What if ... what if it began to fly, to come up the stairs towards her?

She yelled, "Marianne, is that you? Danny! Soo!" And still the buffer moved closer and closer.

She was trapped. She had to pass that buffer to get to the window where they'd come in. But she couldn't go down there, she couldn't take another step. Who was doing this to her?

Nicola stepped back, tried to think what to do. Was there another way out?

Something moved behind her. She didn't want to look, but she had to. Something cold brushed against her cheek.

She swung round, and screamed.

It was a face, twisted and ugly, there in the shadows, watching her.

The teacher, the teacher with the burnt face. Nicola couldn't breathe, couldn't think, just wanted away. She almost cried, "Help me!" like the scream of terror she'd heard earlier. Was this what Soo had seen? Or was it Destiny? How she wished she'd left with Marianne.

She began to run again, run back up the stairs, away from the hum of the buffer in the downstairs corridor, away from that awful face.

She tripped on the steps, hurt her shins, but she didn't stop. Too afraid to stop. In case a cold hand would reach out for her.

Was it behind her still, following her? She couldn't look.

She banged against the swing doors again, and began to back down the corridor. Her eyes never left the doors as they swung, back and forth, almost as if they too had come to life.

What if that face came after her? What if it was floating through the dark? Heading her way. Her teeth were chattering, her hands shaking. She wanted away from here, but how?

There was a sudden sound behind her, a bang that made her jump. It came again, a single tap. Between 1C and the next class-room was a locker. She'd often seen it open, full of books and jotters and boxes, and all the rubbish that teachers had to take away from pupils during lessons.

Her gasp of fear turned to anger. Anger was OK. She knew one of the others – could it be Marianne? – had to be hiding in there.

They were tapping on the door, trying to scare her. They were all trying to scare her.

No way. She ran back up the corridor, to the class-room door, got to the locker and dragged it open.

"Now I've got you!" she shouted.

Books, and brushes, and mops fell out on top of her. She stepped back quickly. A football landed on her head, and she punched it away with her fist. It bounced down the corridor, vanished into the blackness. She heard it slowly come to a stop. Nicola kicked at the books and the brushes. She would not be afraid.

But it was so dark, so silent. And she was so alone. What had happened to her friends?

There was a sound from the darkness at the end of the corridor. Slowly, Nicola turned.

Her spine turned to ice.

The ball was bouncing back down the corridor towards her.

Chapter 10
The Witching Hour

"Who's there?" Nicola called out. But no one answered. And she knew by how hollow her shout sounded that no one was there. Just that ball bouncing towards her. She didn't want it near her. She didn't want it to touch her.

She had one thought – escape. Her eyes darted to 1C. She saw the open door and ran in. As soon as she was inside she slammed the door shut. Then she backed against a desk. She kept on watching the door. She listened to the ball as it bounced past. Held her breath till all was silent again.

Nicola tried to think straight. Someone was out there, doing all this to her. To scare her. Was it one of her friends? Why would her friends do that?

Her plan had been that the new girl would be left alone. The new girl would be afraid.

The wind rattled the old windows, trees swayed and scratched against the glass. "Stop that noise!" Nicola yelled out, and put her hands over her ears to block out the sound. She wished it was morning. Light.

In a moment, she told herself, she would step to the door, pull it open, call out again to see if anyone would answer her.

She would not be afraid. There was nothing to be afraid of. The school was not haunted.

And yet ... she remembered the buffer, and the face in the dark ... and that ball. Someone had to be out there. But was it someone alive – or dead?

They should never have had that séance.

Nicola shivered. She wanted more than anything to go out into that corridor. But her feet felt like blocks of stone. Too heavy to move.

She heard a sound in the distance. The church clock in the town struck twelve.

It was midnight.

The witching hour.

The moment she had planned for the new girl to be alone here.

Not her.

Not Nicola.

It was in this class-room that some evil spirit was meant to appear. 1C. It was a story told in whispers in the school. A figure almost seen, sounds almost heard, always coming from this class-room.

But there was nothing here. Nothing to be afraid of.

It was an empty class-room. With posters, and books and papers on the teacher's desk, a smartboard on the wall ...

She looked up at the smartboard again. It was lit up. And there were new words –

I'm here, Nicola.

Chapter 11
Trapped

Nicola had never been so afraid. It was as if something was holding her here, in this class-room. And she couldn't escape.

She didn't deserve this.

Yes, you do ...

The words in her head made her remember what they'd done to Lana Watt, but she wasn't going to listen to them.

"I don't deserve this!" she screamed out, and this time – this time it was not in her head but for real – someone answered her. There was a soft whisper.

"*Yes, you do,*" someone hissed.

"Is that you, Soo? Is that you?" Nicola would be angry if it was Soo. "You were every bit as bad as me," she said. "Don't kid yourself."

No one answered her. Only the wind. But someone had to be there.

"You've all been talking to that Marianne. And Marianne's suddenly feeling all bad about it."

She wanted someone to answer her. She felt the midnight darkness was closing in on her. She felt more and more trapped. "Why doesn't someone answer me?"

And ... was that a snigger she heard, soft, cruel, laughing at her? At Nicola?

A shadow passed the door. Someone was outside. "Danny!" She called his name. Danny wouldn't do this to her. He was almost her boyfriend, wasn't he? It had to be one of the others doing this to her.

Because if it wasn't one of them, then it must be ...

The stories she'd heard in school. Stories they'd all heard. The teacher in the darkness looking for the care-taker who killed her, the teacher with no face.

She saw a hint of the shadow again, and didn't even think about it. She ran for the door. Pulled it open.

And screamed.

Neatly stacked right outside the door were all the books, the jotters, the boxes from the locker.

Trapping her here in this class-room.

She was gasping for breath. "Someone help me ... please ..."

Her foot caught on a chair. She tripped, fell back. The shadows seemed to be closing in all around her. Almost as if they were sucking her in.

She wanted to faint. That was the only way she would escape from this. But she couldn't faint. She was too scared about what she might see when she opened her eyes again.

Nicola crawled under one of the desks. Drew up her legs, hugged her knees. She was shaking now. Couldn't stop.

Nowhere to run.

It was the foot-steps she heard.

Click, click, click ...

A slow tapping up the corridor.

Not Danny's footsteps, or Sanji's.

It wasn't Soo's trainers. Or Marianne's.

From under the desk all Nicola saw was the shoes as they stopped at the class-room door.

Silly shoes, white, with high heels.

"I'm here, Nicola," someone said.

Chapter 12
Destiny

It was Destiny. But a different Destiny. It wasn't the Destiny who was a nervous, shy new girl – no. The girl standing in the door-way stood straight and tall.

Nicola peeked up to see her. "Destiny, thank heaven it's you," she said.

She crawled out from under the desk. Was this really Destiny? Nicola got to her feet. Her legs were shaking. Destiny's face was in shadow, but Nicola could see her eyes, sunk deep and dark.

Why wasn't she saying anything?

"Did you see any of the rest of them?" Nicola said, and then she began to babble on about the face and the buffer and the ball. And still Destiny said nothing.

"Did you see any of them?" Nicola asked again.

At last Destiny spoke. "They've all gone."

Her voice sounded different, odd and far-away.

"What's wrong with you?" Nicola asked.

"What do you think, Nicola?"

Destiny stepped into the class-room. Nicola moved back, couldn't stop herself from saying, "I didn't know where anyone was. Did you hear me shouting?"

She wanted Destiny to be as afraid as she was. But Destiny didn't look afraid.

Nicola ran her hands through her hair. She should feel better now that she wasn't alone. Why didn't she feel better?

"Where's Marianne? Where's Danny?" Nicola asked.

She expected to hear them running up the corridor any second now.

"They've all gone, Nicola. They've all left you. It's just you and me."

Nicola took another step back. Why was this girl making her so afraid? "What do you mean, they've left me?"

"Not nice being left alone, is it, Nicola?" Destiny said.

"I'm not alone. My friends are here somewhere."

"They've all left you. Sanji and Soo, Danny and Marianne. You're the odd one out. Odd." The way she said that word, "odd", made Nicola feel cold all over. "You were always the odd one out," Destiny went on.

"That's not true!" But Nicola was remembering now how Marianne and Soo were always at each other's houses and not inviting her. How she would see Sanji and Soo and Marianne and Danny sitting together in the cafe, and they never asked her over.

She was always the one left out.

No. No. She pushed those thoughts away.

"What have you done with my friends?" she asked.

"You don't have any friends, Nicola," Destiny said softly. "Not real friends. They do what you want, like they did with Lana Watt. But they don't like you."

"What do you know about Lana Watt?" Nicola asked.

"You drove her crazy. Loopy Lana, isn't that what you called her?"

"How do you know that? Who are you?"

Destiny didn't answer. She said nothing. It was Nicola who spoke next.

"You're the one who's been doing all this," she said. She understood it all now. "You were standing at the smartboard just before we saw the first message. You must have written it. You started the buffer. You bounced the ball back."

"Did I?" Destiny said.

Nicola was remembering now. "And it wasn't me who had the idea of a night in school. It was you. It wasn't me who said, 'Let's have a séance'. It was you. It's you who's been doing all these things ... *you!*"

"Is it?" Destiny asked slowly.

"Yes! You've been trying to scare me!" And now Nicola started to feel angry, not scared any more. It had been Destiny all along, trying to scare her. "Well," Nicola shouted. "It's finished."

"It's not over yet, Nicola."

"Yes it is. My friends will come back for me," Nicola said.

"Will they?"

"Yes, they will! And then we'll make you sorry!"

"Will you, Nicola?"

"Why are you doing this? Who's Lana Watt to you?"

But Destiny didn't answer. All she said was, "It isn't over yet."

She seemed to be moving away from Nicola and out of the class-room. Nicola blinked, and Destiny was gone. Where had she gone?

Nicola was breathing hard. In a moment she would go. Nothing to be afraid of here. She understood now. It had all been Destiny. No ghosts. Next week at school, she would find out why. Then she'd make Destiny sorry.

But "It isn't over yet," Destiny had said. What did she mean?

The room was still. The wind had died.

Then suddenly the class-room door slammed shut again. Nicola jumped.

There was no wind outside anymore. Was there?

Another moment passed. She heard something move in the corner of the room. She didn't want to look. Had to. Something was shifting in the shadows, a shadow itself. Coming to life. A dark shadow, that was all. And yet ...

It began to crawl across the floor towards her.

Nicola's heart was thumping. She saw now it was a woman's shadow, crawling closer and closer. Nicola wanted to run, but she was glued to the spot. Couldn't move. Closer and closer the shadow came. It was almost at her feet now.

Nicola didn't want to see. She tried to close her eyes. But some power made her look. The shadow raised its head. Looked up at Nicola.

And it had no face. There was no face!

And then Nicola started to scream, and scream, and scream.

Chapter 13
All Together Now

She was still screaming when they all ran into 1C. Nicola was curled into a ball under one of the desks. Soo bent down and touched her. Nicola punched at her, looked at her as if she didn't know who she was.

"What happened?" Soo asked.

"She can't answer," Marianne said. "Look at her. She's like someone mad."

Soo looked all around. "Do ... do you think she saw something in here?"

"Serve her right if she did," Marianne said. "Look what she was going to do to Destiny."

"I expect she saw one of her own tricks," Danny said, and he threw the mask on the floor. "I found that on the stairs."

"Do you really think Nicola did all those things? The words on the smartboard, the locked doors?"

"Who else could it be?" Danny said. "She never tells us what her plans are. Just expects us to back her up."

"It wasn't me," Sanji said. "I didn't know anything about that mobile phone or its ring-tone. Still haven't found it." He pulled Soo towards him. "I'm glad I found you, Soo. I was getting freaked out running round this school on my own."

Nicola had stopped screaming. She was crying softly.

"She's lucky we came back for her ... not that we wanted to," Danny said.

"But what did she see in here?" Marianne gripped Danny's hand.

"We have to get her home," Soo said.

"How are we going to tell her mum what happened to her?" Sanji asked. "And where did Destiny go? Why couldn't we find her?"

Marianne had the answer. "Destiny hates us. And who can blame her? Bet she'll be home by now."

"That's where I want to go. Home," Soo said. "Let's get out of here."

Danny pulled out his phone. "I'll call my brother Tony. He's got a car. He'll come and get us."

"If you get a signal," Sanji said.

Danny looked at him. "Phone works now."

They watched Danny's face as he spoke to his brother. "I'll tell you about it when you pick us up," he said.

"We'd better make sure Destiny got home OK," Marianne said.

Danny nodded. He said something into the phone. "Tony, do you know the new girl, Destiny? Do you know where she lives?"

As Danny listened to his brother, his face went white. "What? What do you mean? No. No, that can't be right."

"What is it, Danny?" Marianne asked.

"Tony ... Tony?" He punched the numbers, shook the phone. "We've lost the signal again."

"What did your brother say?" Sanji asked.

Danny shook his head. He sounded shocked. "I don't understand. Tony says ... there is no new girl in the school." He looked from one to the other of them. He spoke the next words slowly. "Did you hear me? Tony said there's no new girl in the school!"

"What's happened here tonight? I don't understand." Soo was breathing hard. "I'm scared. There's too many shadows in this room. Let's get out of here, please. I think we should get out of here *now*!"

Suddenly everything went very still again. They all looked at each other.

And, just at that moment, a gust of wind slammed the class-room door shut.

And Nicola starting to scream again.

Barrington Stoke would like to thank all its readers for commenting on the manuscript before publication and in particular:

Sanna Afzalishamabad

Karin Carter

Katie Chapman

Tess Church

Polly Cross

Georgia Davies

Nathan Davies

Charlotte Daynton

Beatrix Harrison

Adam Ali Hussain

Aaron Lay

Daniel Longley

Lynn Longley

Beth Marshall

Miss Marshall

Antony Maxwell

Robert Maxwell

Kerry Metcalf

Claire Norton

Ellie Preston

Siobhan Riordan

Gareth Rothon

Sian Shields

Charlotte Smith

Benjamin Tennett

Kashif Wahid

Dom Waldock

Adam Walton

Amy Wilson

Olivia Wilson

Become a Consultant!

Would you like to give us feedback on our titles before they are published? Contact us at the email address below – we'd love to hear from you!

info@barringtonstoke.co.uk
www.barringtonstoke.co.uk

Great reads – no problem!

Barrington Stoke books are:

Great stories – from thrillers to comedy to horror, and all by the best writers around!

No hassle – fast reads with no boring bits, and a story that doesn't let go of you till the last page.

Short – the perfect size for a fast, fun read.

We use our own font and paper to make it easier to read our books. And we ask teenagers like you, who want a no-hassle read, to check every book before it's published.

That way, we know for sure that every Barrington Stoke book is a great read for everyone.

Check out www.barringtonstoke.co.uk for more info about Barrington Stoke and our books!

Also by Catherine MacPhail

Sticks and Stones

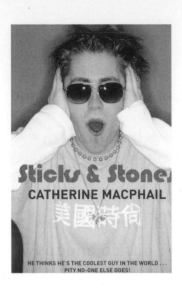

Greg's sure he's the funniest and most popular guy in school. So why does everybody think he's stolen Tony Harris' mobile?
It can't be a set-up. After all, everybody loves him ... don't they?
He's going to need all his brains, and some help, to get him out of this one!

A Kind of Magic

When Nick's best mate Ravi finds a rare fossil on a school trip, Nick's not impressed. But when he sees that this odd object seems to bring good luck to whoever owns it, he wants it for himself.
But is the fossil all it seems to be? And why do bad things start happening to him too?

You can order these books directly from our website at
www.barringtonstoke.co.uk

Fury
by
Elizabeth Kay

The Furies are hunters. They punish people for the crimes of their parents. And now they're coming for Melanie. Her only hope is to find out the dark secrets of her mother's past – before the Furies get their revenge.

Ghosting
by
Keith Gray

Nat and his sister help the living contact the dead. But this time the dead are talking back. And now the screams won't stop ... Someone should have told them there are worse things than ghosts ...

You can order these books directly from our website at
www.barringtonstoke.co.uk